MARVEL

ANT-MAN

MARVEL

ANT-MAN

THE JUNIOR NOVEL

ADAPTED BY CHRIS WYATT

INSPIRED BY MARVEL'S *ANT-MAN*

BASED ON THE SCREENPLAY BY ADAM MCKAY & PAUL RUDD

STORY BY EDGAR WRIGHT & JOE CORNISH

PRODUCED BY KEVIN FEIGE

DIRECTED BY PEYTON REED

LITTLE, BROWN AND COMPANY
New York   Boston

Little, Brown and Company

Hachette Book Group
1290 Avenue of the Americas, New York, NY 10104
Visit us at lb-kids.com

Little, Brown and Company is a division of Hachette Book Group, Inc. The Little, Brown name and logo are trademarks of Hachette Book Group, Inc.

The publisher is not responsible for websites (or their content) that are not owned by the publisher.

First Edition: June 2015

Library of Congress Control Number: 2015936320

ISBN: 978-0-316-25674-2

10 9 8 7 6 5 4 3 2 1

RRD-C

Printed in the United States of America

San Quentin State Prison was the oldest correctional facility in California. Some of the toughest, meanest, and ugliest criminals to ever enter the system had spent time behind San Quentin's bars.

Many of those prisoners were gathered together right now, screaming and cheering as the biggest of them all threw a punch at Scott

Lang. As the fist flew at Scott's face, time seemed to slow down. He watched the knuckles coming, and all he could think about was how much it was going to hurt.

Scott was a very handsome yet boyish-looking man with an easy charm and a casual, friendly way with people. He could usually talk himself out of most situations that threatened to turn violent…but not this one.

Bam! The force of the hit slammed into Scott's jaw, causing him to stumble back. It was only by sheer luck that Scott was able to keep his balance and stay on his feet as he looked up at his attacker.

"Awww, man…" said the scary-looking dude. "I'm going to miss you, Scott."

Scott rubbed his sore jaw and stuck his hand out to shake hands with the brute. "Yeah, I'm going to miss you, too, Peachy. But you guys have

2

the weirdest-going 'good-bye' rituals. I'm going to feel that for weeks!"

Peachy grabbed Scott's outstretched hand and pulled Scott closer, wrapping the much smaller man into a big bear hug!

Each of the other prisoners took turns patting Scott on the back or shaking his hand. He was a nice guy and pretty popular with the other inmates. Everyone was sorry to see him go.

But Scott wasn't sorry. After years of living in a cold gray cell, he had finally done his time, and was going to be free....

Scott's face was still smarting from Peachy's "farewell" as he thanked the guards who ushered him past the banged-up perimeter fence.

Walking out through the gates of San Quentin after years on the inside was one of the greatest feelings of his life. He stopped for a moment to breathe in his first breath of non-prison air.

Everything seemed possible....

Scott looked across the road at a man standing in front of a dented-up old van.

"Look at that familiar face," Scott called out to Luis. "And look at that disgusting van. No way that's street legal."

"Look at that beat-up face," Luis replied warmly. "Let me guess—Peachy?"

"You got it," said Scott, chuckling.

"I've still got a mark from my 'going-away present,' and that was a year ago," said Luis as he raised his chin, showing Scott. Then he kissed his own fist. "But I'm still the only guy who ever knocked him out."

Reaching Luis, Scott gave him a bro hug.

"I miss that guy," said Luis. "How is he?"

"Enormous," Scott replied as two climbed into Luis's van.

Soon they were on the road, headed back to town.

Luis was Scott's old cellmate, and the two had quickly bonded over sports, favorite TV shows, and a mutual hatred of San Quentin's commissary food.

Both Luis and Scott had been in for the same kind of crime, burglary. But Luis's crimes hadn't caused the same nationwide media sensation that Scott's crime had. Plus, Scott's "crimes" always started with the "best intentions"…but that was a whole separate issue.

They'd split a small cell for many months. Luis had been the first to get out, and he

was quick to offer his friend a place to stay after prison. Once their time inside was over, everybody needed a little while to get back on their feet.

Excited to see his old friend after so long, Luis was chatting a mile a minute as he drove along. "It's good to see you, holmes," he said. "I got the couch all set up. You can stay as long as you like. It'll be like old times."

Scott gave Luis a worried glance. "Old times" had been spent locked in a high-security prison. Scott wasn't too interested in things being like "old times."

"And you'll be back on your feet in no time," Luis continued. "I want to introduce you to some good people I met since I got out...skilled people."

Scott knew that "skilled" was Luis's way of

6

saying "great at breaking and entering."

"Whoa," said Scott. "Listen, I did my time, and now I'm going straight. I've got a daughter to think about."

Luis gave Scott a sad look. It was the kind of look you might give a kid who thinks his ice cream's not going to melt.

"Real jobs don't come around too easily for anyone these days, let alone for ex-cons," said Luis. "Even for geniuses like you."

The look in Luis's eyes worried Scott—but he knew that he had to go straight. He couldn't risk being thrown back in prison.

"I've got a master's in electrical engineering," said Scott. "I'm sure I can find a decent job." But the way he said it made Luis think he wasn't really sure and was just trying to convince himself that what he said was true.

"Whatever you say, bro," said Luis noncommittally.

Despite Luis's concerns, as well as his own, within two weeks, Scott had a job.

But it wasn't a great job.

And it didn't require a master's degree in electrical engineering.

It just required little plastic gloves and an ice cream scoop.

The bell rang as another customer walked in.

Scott smiled, and said: "Welcome to our ice cream shop. Can I interest you in our new Smoothie Fruit Blaster?"

"You guys have burgers?" said the rather odd-looking customer.

"What? No. We have ice cream."

"Oh," said the customer, scratching his temple. He paused for a long moment, considering the menu up on the wall before asking, "What about nuggets?"

Scott blinked. "Dude…" was all he managed to say.

Before the customer could ask another dumb question, Dale, Scott's manager—a man overly proud of his modest achievements—poked his head out of the back office. Dale looked at Scott, and asked, "Can I see you in the back, chief?"

Dale was always—*always*—calling people "chief" or "bud" or something. It was probably because he didn't care enough to learn anyone's name.

"Sure thing, Dale," said Scott, pleased to be escaping the weird customer, if nothing else.

Once in Dale's office, Scott removed the gloves he had to wear when handling the ice cream. They made smacking noises as they came off.

"Pull up a chair," said Dale, pointing at the flimsy plastic one across from the cluttered desk. Scott sat in it and looked at his manager expectantly.

Dale returned a vacuous smile.

"Three years in San Quentin, huh?" asked Dale.

Scott was shocked and disappointed. "You found out?"

Dale nodded seriously. "This is an ice cream shop—we take this stuff pretty seriously."

"Look, I'm sorry I lied on my application, but no one would hire me," said Scott quickly and desperately. "It wasn't a violent crime, and I'm a good worker."

Dale looked over a thick stack of papers on his desk. "Says on the report it was breaking and entering...and grand larceny?"

Scott blinked. "Wow, that's a thorough report."

Dale looked up as if he was trying to remember something. "Wait...Scott Lang? Were you the guy that robbed that billionaire?"

"Yeah, that would be me," said Scott sheepishly.

A smile sprang to Dale's lips. "You were on the news! Man, you've got guts! Respect!"

Scott was relieved. Maybe this was going to go better than he'd thought...."So, does that mean you can give me another chance? I promise I won't let you down."

Dale instantly turned serious. "Sorry, no can do. Gotta fire you, champ. But you know what? I'll let you grab a Smoothie Fruit Blaster on your way out...."

Scott shrugged. A free smoothie…At least that was something. It was more than he had gotten at all the other places where he had applied for a job.

He headed back to the front of the shop. As he did, he heard Dale call after him, "…only half price!"

A half-free smoothie. OK…It was *half* of something.

CHAPTER 2

Scott sipped on his Smoothie Fruit Blaster as he walked through the roughest neighborhood he'd ever seen. He'd used sandpaper that he thought was less rough. Seriously, he'd felt safer back when he was in prison.

Scott climbed several flights of stairs to get to Luis's apartment. The elevator was out, of course, because it was always out. So Scott

tromped past the apartment with the Latina lady and her pretty daughter, and past the weird ravers who were always blasting electronica, and past the old man with the yappy little dog. When the dog barked at him, he just said to it, "Down, killer."

Reaching Luis's door, he unlocked it. Then unlocked the second lock. Then the third. As he unlocked the final lock, Scott wondered if there were enough locks, and considered talking to Luis about getting a few more.

As soon as he pushed open the door, he was hit with the delicious aroma of cooking.

"Scotty, what're you doing here?" shouted Luis from across the room. "I thought you had work." Luis was fiddling with something on the counter that Scott couldn't see.

"I did. I got fired," Scott said, taking a bitter

14

sip of his sweet smoothie. "They found out who I really am."

Luis nodded knowingly. "See, I told you, man. Don't mess with ice cream shops, dude. They always find out."

"It's true," added another voice. "Cold ice cream, cold hearts."

Scott turned to see two other guys in Luis's apartment, both strangers to him. Luis introduced Dave, Luis's longtime friend who used to steal from houses during the day, when the owners were at work. Dave was a pretty good guy, Luis claimed, when he wasn't stealing from you—and he was legendary in the local criminal community for his skills as a getaway driver.

The other guy was about Scott's age, and he too had the air of the ex-con about him, but Luis didn't introduce him immediately.

"Here's the good news," said Luis. "It's waffle Thursday. You want a waffle?" Luis held up a measuring cup filled with batter, and Scott could now see what Luis had been fiddling with when Scott came in—a waffle iron.

Scott smiled. So that was what he smelled. "Sure, I'll take a waffle!" he said enthusiastically. Scott knew from long experience that *everything*, even getting fired, seemed better after eating a waffle.

"It's hard to find work with a record," said the guy Scott hadn't met. "I used my computer skill to generate three hundred false IDs, and now I can't even get a job selling electronics at a big-box store." The man spoke with a heavy foreign accent that Scott had trouble identifying. It was a kind of Russian accent.

"That's brutal," said Scott, shaking his head. "Who are you, by the way?"

Luis answered while pulling a fresh waffle off the iron, putting it on a paper plate, and covering it with powdered sugar. "This is Kurt," he said, nodding in the direction of his friend. "Kurt was in Folsom for five years. Identity theft. He's a wizard with a laptop. Kurt, meet Scott, my ex–cell mate."

Dave spoke up, addressing Kurt. "Scott's the guy who robbed Vista Corp's CEO. He's a heavy player."

Scott scoffed at this, responding while forking a bite of waffle into his mouth. "I'm hardly a 'heavy player,'" Scott said, as he chewed on waffle—crispy outside, doughy inside…great.

"What do you mean 'hardly'?" Luis asked

Scott before turning back to Kurt. "Check it out. My homeboy Scott actually worked for Vista Corp. But then he finds out they were up to some shady stuff...."

Kurt looked intrigued. "What was the nature of their shade?"

"You don't know Vista Corp?" asked Dave. "What planet are you from?"

Kurt shrugged. "I don't have TV in my country," he said, as if that explained everything.

"What? The whole country?" asked Dave.

Kurt nodded. "We sell it for meat," he said.

Everyone looked at Kurt for a second, wondering if he was joking or not. What country was he supposed to be from? But it wasn't worth asking, so Luis just moved on.

"Vista Corp was overcharging customers," Luis said. "It added up to millions. He"—Luis

said, pointing at Scott—"blows the whistle, and they fire him."

Kurt looked at Scott, asking, "Why you not go to the press?"

"I did," Scott said, then shrugged. "But Vista was too powerful. There was an investigation and they covered it up. I became 'a disgruntled former employee trying to extort a hard-working corporation.'"

"So then what does he do?" asks Luis rhetorically, while pouring the batter for another waffle. He loved telling this story. "He decrypts their security system and transfers millions back to the people they stole it from!"

Suddenly, a light turned on for Kurt. "Oh, wait.... The Vista job. I heard about this robbery!"

Scott was quick to correct him. "Technically, I didn't rob them. Robbing involves threat. I burgled them…I hate violence. I'm more of a cat burglar."

"He ripped off every member of the board," said Luis proudly. "It was a major score!"

Thinking about the little guy striking back against the corporate giants, Luis, Kurt, and Dave were all smiles. Only Scott wasn't smiling.

Scott could remember it all like it was yesterday. The shock at finding out the company was so crooked, the disappointment at learning the company was powerful enough to make the newspapers and the police look the other way. The outrage he'd felt at finding himself—who had done nothing wrong—the subject of a campaign designed to muscle him into silence. The triumph of getting even, and finally the tragedy of what it had all meant to his young family.

"They ruined me," he said. "I had a family to support."

"But then he snuck into the CEO's house!" continued Dave.

"He burgled five million in cash and jewelry for himself," added Luis.

"He posted all the CEO's bank records online!" said Dave.

"Then drove the dude's fancy car into his swimming pool!" finished Luis.

Scott shrugged again. "I got carried away."

The others looked at Scott, feeling like they were in the presence of a legend. Scott felt their eyes on him, and said, "I'm not really that way, though." He looked away awkwardly.

Luis laughed. "What about those jobs you pulled before Vista?"

"That was a long time ago," said Scott.

"And I'm not proud of it."

Scott had pulled off a few petty thefts in the distant past, starting when he was a teenager. He had always been good with machines, which is what led him to a career in electrical engineering; so many other people were so bad with machines. So, in his youth, it was hard to resist the temptation to use his knowledge to his own advantage. It was never a big deal, just little stuff. Still, he regretted it. If he hadn't made those mistakes, maybe he wouldn't have made the big mistake he had with the Vista CEO.

By now, Luis had handed waffles all around, and the four ex-cons each took bites of their sweet, golden-brown goodness. While chewing, each thought about past jobs, and how sweet those had been, too.

"These are the best waffles ever made," Luis didn't mind saying. No one disagreed with him.

Suddenly, Scott eyed Luis suspiciously. "Wait…Why are you in such a good mood?"

Luis, Kurt, and Dave all shared a significant look, like they were all in on some inside information. They smiled among themselves, a pleasantly guilty look on their faces.

Luis paused for a second, trying to think how best to start his story. "So," he finally began, "last week, my cousin was talking to this guy, and—"

"No way!" Scott practically shouted. He didn't need to hear the rest of the story. He could tell where this was going. Luis clearly had some idea for a criminal enterprise, based on some weird, dodgy, secondhand info.

"Come on!" implored Luis, trying to appeal to Scott's sense of social justice. "This fits your MO.

Some retired gazillionaire living off his golden parachute!"

"I told you—I'm done," said Scott, shaking his head. "I'm not doing anything else illegal ever again."

This time the others all shared a disappointed look.

"But I will have another waffle," Scott said, holding out his plate.

As Luis forked one up, he proudly proclaimed, "There are three things I do well…I love, I rob, and I make waffles."

None of them noticed the ant sitting on the kitchen counter watching them. After all, why should they notice a tiny ant…?

Except this one was special.

This one was equipped with an almost microscopic video camera. The high-tech audio-

visual recording equipment was pointed right at Scott, Luis, and their friends.

And since the ant-cam's little red Record light was on, everything the ant was seeing and hearing, everything Scott was doing and saying, must have been transmitting to some receiver somewhere....

Hope Van Dyne was smart, young, and beautiful, but she didn't flaunt her looks. She was no-nonsense, and tough as nails when she needed to be. She had a talent for realizing when she was being lied to, and another talent for hiding her thoughts and emotions. She knew how to play her cards close to her vest. In fact, that was her default setting.

She sat at the table in the elegant restaurant, looking over at her dining companion, Darren Cross, as he handed her a tablet computer. After a beat, she accepted the device and looked at it, pressing the triangular Play button.

The black screen suddenly jumped to life, showing footage of the 1969 Apollo 11 moon landing. Neil Armstrong, clad in his spacesuit, said, "That's one small step for man, one giant leap for mankind" as he set foot on lunar soil for the first time in history.

A voice-over ran on top of the footage. "Just as human civilization began with a single stop," said the narrator as the image quickly transitioned to a slick CGI shot of cavemen gathering around a fire—then smoothly pulled back to show the formation of an ancient city in the distance.

"And the modern age began with one bright

idea," intoned the narrator over images of an ancient Mesopotamian carving the first wheel from stone—then that first wheel morphed into one of many wheels on a modern vehicle assembly line.

Hope raised an eyebrow. The video was laying it on a little thick. As she watched, the assembly line wheels transitioned into a giant cog. The camera then pulled back to reveal that the cog was just one of the many inside the clock mechanism that ran London's famous Big Ben.

The images were clearly designed to inspire people and show them how good ideas could grow to culture-shaping proportions.

"Mankind's achievements are the sum total of their parts," continued the narrator. "They're small steps adding up to giant leaps. From Big Ben to the big bang…it's the tiny ingredients

that make the magic." As the narrator said this, the screen showed subatomic particles but then pulled back at hyper-speed to show a shot of the entire galaxy.

Then came the part of the video that Hope was most dreading. She watched herself walk onto the screen as a title appeared: HOPE VAN DYNE — PYM TECH.

"Pym Tech is more than a company," Hope heard herself saying. "It's a family, working together at the forefront of the chemical energy industry, to craft technologies with applications varying from the personal…to the universal."

When the Hope on screen said "personal," the image cut to a wounded veteran holding a little baby by means of artificial limbs.

"From the flexible alloys used in lightweight prosthetic limbs…"

The image changed again, this time showing a collage of different alternative energy plants: a large wind farm, a field of solar panels, and a hydroelectric dam.

"...to the world's most promising alternative energy platforms..."

Now the video cut to Hope standing in a research lab. "...We want to bring you the technologies of tomorrow."

The video quickly cut to a suited man standing against a black background. The man turned to face the camera as the narrator announced him. "And now, our visionary CEO—Darren Cross."

In the restaurant, the real Darren Cross eagerly watched Hope's reaction as the footage of him played on the screen. She gave no visible response.

On the table, the prerecorded Darren Cross

gazed out, as if looking at his anticipated future audience, and said: "At Pym Technologies, big things come from small beginnings."

The video cut out, and the real Hope looked up at the real Darren.

"What do you think?" he asked expectantly.

"It certainly sends a message," said Hope. It was a sentence perfectly crafted to express as little of an actual opinion as possible.

Expecting more, Darren kept his eyes trained on Hope.

"Stop looking at me like that," said Hope after a moment.

"I just want to make sure everything is to your liking," said Darren.

Hope's face remained blank. "You know me. I'd be happy with a cheeseburger."

"I love that about you," Darren said

enthusiastically. "You stay focused on the things that matter. Sure, these fancy things are nice. But what really matters is the work...the science... the innovation. Pym Tech is on the verge of changing the world. And I owe much of that to you. You've been a revelation. And I want you to know, from the bottom of my heart...I appreciate you."

It took all of Hope's strength not to roll her eyes at this. "I'm just grateful to be a part of it."

Darren slipped his hand across the table and reached out to Hope. But Hope didn't move her hand to meet his, which forced Darren to rise out of his seat a little bit to do an awkward stretch across the table in order to place his hand tenderly on hers.

After a moment, Darren relaxed and raised his glass. "To gratitude," he said.

Hope raised her glass, clinking it with his and hoping he was finally done talking.

No such luck.

After taking a quick sip, Darren began again. "I've been thinking about gratitude a lot recently. And today, during my morning meditation, something interesting occurred to me. I think it might apply to you."

"What might that be?"

"Gratitude can also be forgiveness. I've spent years carrying around my anger for Hank Pym." Darren's voice did, indeed, have a hint of angry emotion creeping into it. "He made me feel like I wasn't even worth the neutron poisons at the back end of a nuclear fuel cycle, even though I devoted my genius to him when I could have worked anywhere. I chose my mentor poorly… and you didn't even have a choice. It's a shame

what we had to do. But he forced our hand, didn't he?"

Darren had clearly worked himself up talking about something that struck a nerve for him. But he caught himself and tried to calm down. He inhaled and exhaled with deliberation.

"We shouldn't be angry about it. We should be grateful. His failures as a mentor, and as a man, forced us to spread our wings."

Hope leveled a frank look at Darren.

"You're a success, Darren," Hope said. "You deserve everything that's coming your way."

If there was a hint of a veiled threat in Hope's words, Darren didn't detect it. Instead, he was touched, his eyes tearing up a little bit. He leaned back in his seat, satisfied.

Hope was so focused on Darren's smug face

that she didn't hear the loud backfire that came from a passing van outside.

L uis had loaned his van to Scott for a couple of hours. So far it had backfired five times, once so loudly that a crowd of pedestrians all ducked, fearing gunfire.

But Scott coaxed the broken-down vehicle all the way out to a suburban neighborhood on the outskirts of the city, where he pulled onto a side street and parked. Carrying a poorly wrapped birthday gift, he got out of the van and walked up to a house.

Without knocking, Scott stepped right through the doorway into a brightly decorated child's birthday party. Kids were everywhere,

jumping around, playing with balloons, and dancing to child-friendly tunes deejayed by somebody's dad. There was a table set up in the corner, where kids were participating in a messy craft project involving lots of paint and glue.

"Daddy!" squealed a little girl with delight. Scott turned to see his seven-year-old daughter, Cassie, running at him. He opened his arms, letting her run into them. Father and daughter shared a big hug. Scott smiled, feeling her little arms around him. This was what he'd been missing. This was what he lived for.

"Happy birthday, peanut," Scott said to Cassie when they finally broke their hug. "Sorry I'm late. I didn't know what time the party started."

"He didn't know, because he didn't get an invitation," a gruff male voice said.

Scott looked up to see Jim Paxton. Paxton was

big and tough. He was a cop entirely made of muscles, and had a neck as thick as a tree. Paxton was Cassie's soon-to-be-stepdad, and he was no fan of Scott's.

He glowered at Scott, and Scott returned a dirty look back at him.

"Well, I couldn't miss my little girl's birthday party!" said Scott to Cassie brightly, ignoring the waves of aggression coming his way from Paxton.

Cassie jumped, shouting excitedly, "I'm going to tell Mommy you're here!"

As she ran off, Paxton moved close to Scott, and growled, "No one wants you here, Lang."

"Cassie does," Scott said passively.

But behind his back, Scott could hear two of the other parents whispering to each other. "That's *him*. Can you believe it? The nerve.

He's a total deadbeat dad." Scott's cheeks burned with shame.

Paxton squinted at Scott and got even closer, right up in Scott's face. "You haven't paid a dime of child support. Legally, you're not even allowed to be here. If I wanted to arrest you right now, I could...."

Scott looked up at the police officer, who was almost a full head taller than him. Scott had promised himself he'd never get arrested again. Was he going to break that promise now? At his own little girl's birthday party?

Scott kept returning Paxton's glare, not blinking, but also wondering if they'd kept his old cell at San Quentin open.

CHAPTER 4

Scott watched Paxton's eyes, trying to guess what the off-duty cop was going to do next. Was this guy really going to arrest him in front of his own daughter at her birthday party? It seemed like a real possibility....

"Mommy was so happy you were here that she choked on her drink," shouted Cassie, running back up to Scott.

As soon as Cassie got close, Paxton instinctively backed down. It looked like he wasn't going to run Scott in after all.

Scott turned back to his little girl. "Guess who this present is for!" he said, holding out the terribly wrapped package.

"Can I open it now?" she asked excitedly.

"Of course you can, honey. It's your birthday!" Scott answered.

Cassie tore off the paper to reveal the strangest-looking stuffed animal she had ever seen. It was a fluffy, orange...rabbit? Or possibly a cat. It was hard to tell. When Cassie squeezed it, it squeaked, "I love you" in a weird, high voice.

"What is it?" asked Cassie.

"I have no idea," admitted Scott. "I found it in a bodega on Grant and I thought it was perfect... so bizarre!"

Cassie hugged the ugly little rabbit/cat thing. "I love it! It's my favorite present!" she squealed. "Can I go show my friends what my daddy got me?"

Paxton stepped in as if Cassie had asked him the question. "Sure, Cassie. Go ahead, honey."

The little girl ran off.

Scott turned to Paxton, saying, "The child support is coming. It's hard to find work with a criminal record."

Paxton sneered. "You're the genius, right? You'll think of something."

Before Scott could reply, a familiar voice came from behind him. "Scott?"

Scott turned to see his ex-wife, still as gorgeous as the day he married her.

"Hi, Maggie," he said sheepishly. Involuntarily, his heart started beating faster.

"You can't do this. You can't just show up whenever you want to," said Maggie. She was clearly angry but aware of the room full of people around her and trying to keep it contained. "It's too hard on us…all of us."

That hurt.

"She's my daughter, Maggie," Scott replied, a pained expression on his face.

Paxton stepped in again. "You don't know the first thing about being a real father."

Ignoring Paxton, Scott looked directly at his ex. "Maggie, I tell you this as a friend, and as the mother of my child. Your fiancé is a real jerk."

Paxton didn't like that. "You're making a fool out of yourself here, Lang!"

But Maggie turned to Paxton. "Can you give us a minute here, Jim?"

Paxton eyed Scott but backed off like Maggie asked.

"Really, Maggie," said Scott as soon as Paxton was out of earshot, "you had to get engaged to a cop?"

"He can be a little overprotective," Maggie admitted, "but he's a good man. And I'll tell you one thing he's not…a crook."

"Neither am I. I stole from crooks. And I was good at it. Remember?"

"Yeah, I remember," Maggie returned. "I also remember the night I told you I was pregnant. We agreed then and there that you'd give all that up. You made a promise, and you broke it."

"One time!" said Scott. "And these guys had it coming. My intentions were good."

"Intentions don't matter. Actions do. I know love is supposed to be unconditional, but that

was my one condition. Your actions destroyed this family. You put your own sense of backwards justice before your daughter's well-being." Maggie stopped and looked at him. "You're her hero, Scott...and you used to be mine."

That hurt, too.

"I missed so much time," Scott said, imploringly. "I need to see her, Maggie."

Maggie thought for a second before saying, "Then you need to get off your friend's couch and hold down a job. Get a reasonable apartment in a safe neighborhood. Pay child support. Be an honest man. Become the person Cassie already thinks you are."

Scott opened his mouth to reply, but Maggie kept going. "I don't want to shut you out, Scott, but I'll do everything I can to protect her. Get your act together. Then maybe we'll see about visitation."

She paused, looking him over as if trying to figure him out.

"You're the smartest man I know, so quit being so stupid." And with that, Maggie, overcome with emotion, quickly left the room.

Within seconds, Paxton was back at Scott's elbow. "You happy now?" he asked.

Another off-duty policeman, Paxton's partner, Gale, came up behind him. "Everything all right here?" he asked Paxton.

"Just Cassie's biological," Paxton replied.

"Oh, the convict? Is he supposed to be here?"

Scott turned to Paxton. He knew Paxton didn't have a lot of pity for him, but he had to try.

"Can I just say good-bye to Cassie?" he asked.

Paxton seemed surprised that Scott would even ask. He thought about it for a moment before saying, "Fine. Five minutes. Not for you, for her."

Scott shuffled away in search of Cassie. Paxton and Gale followed behind him like store clerks keeping a close eye on a possible shoplifter.

In another part of the house, Scott saw Cassie talking to some of her friends, showing off the toy he'd given her. She was so precious to him. It was killing Scott to think that he'd have to leave her here, not knowing when he might see her next.

He approached her, pulled her aside, and explained that he was going to have to leave. She didn't like that.

"Why can't you be around more, Daddy?" she asked.

"It's complicated, peanut," he said. How

could he explain it all to her?

"I want to see you more," she insisted. "I miss seeing you."

"I miss you, too, sweetheart," said Scott. "I'm just trying to find a job and figure some stuff out, and when I do, I'll see you soooo much!"

Cassie smiled at this. "That's my dream. Cause you know what?"

She squeezed the rabbitlike toy, and it croaked out, "I love you."

Scott chuckled. "Oh man, how weird and great is that?"

"So weird and great," Cassie confirmed.

She squeezed it again, giggling at the strangled words. Scott tried to do an impression of the thing, and that just got Cassie laughing more. But when Scott looked up, he could see Paxton tapping his watch.... Time to go.

Cassie walked out front, standing next to Paxton as she watched Scott climb into Luis's van. As he drove off, Scott hit the van's horn, which played a bizarre little tune.

Cassie smiled at this, the look on her face saying, "Yep, that's my dad."

Scott drove from Maggie's house back through town toward Luis's apartment. He didn't think much about it as he passed the Pym Tech laboratories building. He didn't even notice the lambs that were being brought inside from the loading dock in the back.

Up in one of the labs, Darren Cross stood next to Hope Van Dyne, watching as several technicians worked at various stations. One of the lambs was

being brought in and walked up to a platform.

Seeing the lamb, Hope turned to Darren. "I thought we were starting with mice," she said.

"What's the difference?" said Darren simply. "Commence experiment 34-C. Organic atomic reduction."

A robotic arm positioned itself over the lamb and sprayed a small quantity of formula.

The lamb instantly started shrinking, but soon burst into a blob of goo that twitched for a moment before becoming still.

Hope was horrified!

Darren didn't seem bothered by the fate of the animal he'd just razed, but he was frustrated that the experiment wasn't a success. "Experiment 34-C...unsuccessful," he said.

Hope started to say something. "Maybe we should..."

But Darren cut her off. "Shrinking organic tissue is the centerpiece of this technology. I can't go to the buyers with half of a breakthrough," he said, looking at her. Then he turned to his lab techs, and commanded, "Sanitize the workstation, then bring in subject 35-C."

Back in the parking lot of Luis's building, Scott sat alone in the van. He was writing in ballpoint pen on the back of an old paper bag he'd found on the floorboards.

He needed to figure out what to do next, so, being an engineer, he tried working it out as an equation.

He started by adding the amount he'd need for rent on an apartment to the amount he'd

need for a security deposit. Then he divided that amount by how much he could make per hour at a minimum wage job and begin paying child support. The result would tell him how many days until he could see Cassie again.

When he did the calculation it came out to 381 days....

More than a year before he could see his own child?

No, that was too long.

It was unacceptable.

He was going to have to try something else....

Getting out of the van, he went into the apartment building.

When he walked into the apartment, Luis and Dave were there playing video games. Nearby, Kurt was working on his computer. He was always working on his computer.

"Hey, hotshot," said Luis, not looking up as Scott came in the door. "How'd it go with your daughter?"

Scott gave them all a serious look, then said, "I want to talk about that tip you had."

They all jumped to their feet, Luis and Dave's game, so absorbing moments before, instantly forgotten.

"Oh yeah, it's *on*!" yelled Luis.

"Man, I love stealing stuff," shouted Dave.

"This is excellent, yes?" asked Kurt.

"Stop!" said Scott. "First, you need to tell me exactly where it came from. It needs to be solid."

So Luis started to tell him the story....

Luis and his cousin Ernesto were checking out a party downtown, which was turning out to be pretty lame. But Ernesto told Luis about this girl Emily who they both used to kick it with when they were little. In fact, Emily was the first girl Luis had ever kissed—but that wasn't important.

It seemed that Emily was working as a housekeeper and dating Ernesto's softball teammate Carlos. Emily told Carlos all about this weird old guy she cleaned for. Some aging big-shot CEO who was retired now and who was totally loaded.

Ernesto told Carlos how the old guy had a huge safe sitting there in the basement, just waiting. Big beautiful house, massive safe underground. There had to be something prime inside.

"I'm telling you all this because you've got mad thieving skills," Ernesto told Luis. "Maybe what's in that safe should belong to you."

When Luis got to the end of his story, Scott asked, "Did Emily tell Carlos what kind of safe it was?"

"Nah, dog," said Luis. "She just said it looked

super legit, and that whatever he had in there had to be good."

Kurt looked at Scott. "Not knowing the kind of safe. This is a problem, no?"

"No...not too much of one," said Scott.

Waiting, the others looked at Scott.

"So, are you in or what?" asked Luis.

Scott considered for another beat. The others held their breath.

"Yeah. I'm in," Scott said finally. "But first, I need to get inside and see what we're dealing with."

Luis smiled. "Should we 'fix the cable'?" he asked.

Scott nodded but then happened to notice several ants, all standing in a straight line, their heads up as if they were looking right at them.

"Luis," he said. "I think you have an ant

problem...a really weird one."

Luis didn't bother looking over. "Rats and roaches are a problem. Who cares about ants? We've got bigger things to worry about. Let's get to work."

According to the mail in the mailbox, the house belonged to someone named Dr. Henry Pym. The name rang a bell for Scott, but he didn't worry too much about it. This Dr. Pym did have excellent taste in homes, however. It was a beautifully appointed classic Victorian house.

Luis jumped the fence, got close to the house without being seen, and cut the cable line.

Inside, unseen by Scott and Luis, Dr. Pym himself sat in front of the TV, watching as

it blinked off. He didn't react with surprise. Instead, he just took another sip of his drink.

Scott waited a few minutes before pressing the buzzer on the intercom set in Pym's security gate.

The old man's voice, sheathed in static, burst out of the intercom speaker sharply. "Who is it?"

"Good afternoon, sir. Grady here, from Bayside Cable," said Scott into the intercom. He was dressed in a uniform that fit the role he was playing. "We've detected an outage in your area."

"My cable's out!" shouted the voice of the old man.

"Yes, I'm very sorry, sir. But luckily, I had my truck in the neighborhood, so I came right over to fix it up."

"Well…are you going to fix it?" asked the voice. "The game is on!"

"Wouldn't want you to miss that. Can you buzz me in?"

There was a long pause, then, "Hang on, I'll buzz you in?" Dr. Pym seemed easily confused.

A long buzz sounded as the gate popped open.

Scott approached the front door to see the old man, Dr. Pym, standing in the doorway. He wore a robe, horn-rimmed glasses, and a large, obvious hearing aid. He held a glass in one hand, a cane in the other, and he eyeballed Scott sharply as he came up the sidewalk.

"Come in," said Pym.

Pym turned and walked into the house with a noticeable limp and a slight stoop.

As he walked inside, Scott scanned the place with an experienced criminal's eye. He noted the security pad and the motion detectors on the windows. "This shouldn't take more than a

couple of minutes. Where's your TV?" he asked.

"I suppose you want to know where the TV is," said the old man.

"You took the words right out of my mouth," said Scott, giving Pym a bright, patient smile. Scott noticed some pictures on the wall of Pym with military personnel. "I see you're a military man. See any action?"

"Couple of small skirmishes," answered Pym.

Scott noticed the door to the basement. It was open, with some keys hanging out of the lock. Scott moved in the direction of the door, saying, "The main cable line's through the basement. I'd love to check it out."

"I'm sure you would," said Pym.

"What's that?" asked Scott.

"The cable lines come in through the living room," said Pym, pointing.

"Oh…perfect!" said Scott. "Look at that. You know my business better than me."

"I doubt that," said Pym, shaking his head.

The pair walked into the front room. The curtains were drawn, leaving the room in semidarkness. Scott saw that the room was cluttered, and featured a very old-school swirling-patterned wallpaper of a type that hadn't been in style for decades. All of the room's furniture pointed toward a very old and very large TV.

Scott moved toward one of the curtains, opening it while saying, "I'm going to need a little light to work."

As the light streamed in, Scott discovered that all the clutter was made up of strange, mysterious, and in some cases very valuable-looking artifacts from all over the world. Chinese vases, African masks, gold coins in cases, and other things that

might have looked at home in the display cases of distinguished museums.

"Wow, you're quite a collector," said Scott, looking around. "What's the story with all this stuff?"

"Just junk," said Pym, shrugging and taking another drink.

They clearly weren't just junk. If they were sold, a family of five could probably live off the profits for a year. But they seemed to be meaningless to the old man.

Scott moved to the TV and started tinkering with the cable box, pretending to fix it while actually installing a small camera. While working, Scott looked over and saw an old newspaper featuring a picture of Pym in a suit standing with Darren Cross, his arm proudly around the younger man. The headline read,

"Teen prodigy is the youngest-ever employee."

"Is that your son?" asked Scott, nodding at the picture.

"No, it is not." Pym's voice had a certain finality to it, indicating that he didn't wish to discuss the matter further.

On another wall was a picture of Pym with who must have been his wife and baby girl. "You have a beautiful family," said Scott.

Pym said nothing, preferring to allow an awkward silence to fill the room.

Soon Scott "finished work" on the cable box. "Well, I think I've fixed the problem. Let me just run outside."

Scott excused himself from the room, then ducked back in minutes later. "Should be good now."

Pym punched a button on his remote control.

The TV jumped back to life, a baseball game coming on just as the player at bat hit a long drive.

"Aha! It works," grunted Pym, pleased.

"My pleasure," said Scott. "It was just a power surge."

"It was probably just a power surge," said Pym.

Pym walked Scott to the door, but as Scott was heading out, Pym caught him by the elbow.

"Listen," he said, seeming to get serious, "don't let anyone tell you that you don't have anything to offer, son. Manual labor has its place, and you clearly know your trade."

And with that, Pym produced a shiny new quarter, presented it to Scott while smiling beneficently, as if he were handing over a massive tip.

Scott tried to hide his extreme disdain.

"Thank you, sir, but that's not necessary. I'll let you get back."

"I'm watching the game. I've only got fifty thousand dollars riding on it, but little meaningless wagers make everything more fun, don't you think?"

Scott's smile tightened. This guy threw around cash like it was nothing, but he gave the people who helped him quarters. Fifty thousand dollars would be more than enough to set him up with an apartment, get him back on his feet, and back into Cassie's life…but this guy threw it away on a casual sports bet like it was meaningless.

Luis was right. This was exactly the kind of guy Scott liked to target.

"If you say so, sir," Scott finally said. "Well,

if you have any other issues, feel free to give us a call."

"Oh, I absolutely will," said Pym. "You seem very good at what you do." He smiled and then shut the door in Scott's face.

If Scott had any doubts about targeting this guy for a burglary, they were gone.

CHAPTER 6

Over the next several days, Luis's apartment was a hive of activity as Scott directed the preparations for the heist. Luis had the job of cruising the local electronics stores and acquiring components. He also hit up a locksmith shop, pulling together a box of important supplies.

Kurt had to spend a half day sitting outside an industrial laundry facility waiting for the prime moment to sneak up and grab a uniform out of the large roller bins that were always being moved around the loading bay. Finally, when he got the chance, he walked away with the uniform of a communications technician for a company called Tricomm. That would be his cover.

Dave was responsible for getting a new license plate without any connection to criminal activity for the van. He made his way through the parking lot of a shopping mall and, when no one was looking, stole what he needed.

Back at the apartment, Luis handed off the electrical components to Kurt, who inspected them, then, pleased, started to assemble them together. Simultaneously, Dave, who was going to be the getaway driver, used Internet printouts to map multiple escape routes in case they were

needed. He was going to have to drive each one several times to familiarize himself with the roads.

Finally, everything was ready, everything was planned.

That evening it was "go time."

Luis parked the van a few blocks from the Pym mansion.

Kurt hopped out of the van and scaled the telephone pole that held the lines that led into the house. Since he was wearing his stolen Tricomm uniform, any passersby would assume he was just a technician doing maintenance on the line. But that was the total opposite of the truth. Kurt carefully installed a wireless device to the junction box, blocking the circuit.

When it was done, Kurt spoke to the others over his headset. "Landlines cut, cell signals jammed. No one will be making a distress call tonight," he said.

Down in the van, Dave sat at the wheel, ready to scram at a moment's notice. Luis was in the passenger seat, and ran a quick test of the headsets that, like Kurt, they were all wearing.

"Comm check," said Luis into the headset.

"Check," echoed Scott from the backseat.

"Check," confirmed Dave.

Luis looked at Scott in the backseat. "If it goes south in there, we'll know. We got your back."

"Don't worry," said Scott. "That's not going to happen."

Scott pulled his hood over his head and stepped out of the van.

Luis smiled. "I like it when he gets cocky," he said to Dave. "I'm telling you, he's the real deal."

Slipping up to the grounds of the Pym house,

Scott easily scaled the gate, and then climbed up the outer wall, using gutters and drainpipes to pull himself all the way up to an alarm box hanging near the top of the second story. Hanging on to the wall with one hand, Scott opened the box with the other and flipped a switch inside it.

"All right," he said over the headset. "The window detectors are deactivated."

Luis's voice crackled back a response in his headset. "We're through first position. One down, two to go. You're doing good."

Scott silently slid down one of the drainpipes and entered the house by jimmying open a back window. He slipped quietly through the halls, making his way to the kitchen, where he picked up a set of keys—the one he'd seen before, hanging out of the lock to the basement door.

Scott used the keys and unlocked the basement door, pulling it open.

"You should be moving into second position," said Luis's voice in the headset.

Scott looked at what was in front of him—it was another door. He hadn't expected that. He inspected the security panel.

"There's a fingerprint lock on the door," said Scott to Luis.

"Oh, man. Are we screwed?"

"Not necessarily," said Scott, looking around the kitchen.

"You going to try a homemade workaround?" asked Luis.

Scott riffled through the kitchen drawers until he found clear tape, fast-acting glue, and a lighter. He placed a stretch of tape on a brass doorknob leading into the kitchen, then lifted it

back off carefully. Looking closely at the tape, he could see that he'd lifted an almost complete fingerprint off the metal of the knob.

Next, Scott poured some of the glue onto the tape, which solidified around the ridges of the print. Finally, he used the lighter to gently heat the bottom of the tape. Under the heat, the glue on the print started to harden and rise up off the tape's surface.

Ta-da! Scott had a 3-D copy of the fingerprint. He just hoped it was really Pym's and didn't belong to some random housekeeper or cook.

Scott applied the tape to the fingerprint scanner on the second metal door's security panel.

Beep...Click. The door sprang open.

"I'm in," said Scott triumphantly.

Over the headset, Scott could hear the others cheering him.

"Green light, baby!" shouted Luis. "Seventeen minutes and thirty seconds left on the clock. You're ahead of schedule."

"No alarms at all," reported Kurt.

Back in the car, Dave turned to Luis, telling him, "You're right; your man is good."

Once down in the basement, Scott came face-to-face with the safe Luis had heard so much about. Only it wasn't just a safe; it was a vault.

"What are we looking at?" asked Luis.

"They weren't kidding about the safe. It's serious."

"How serious we talkin' here?"

"It's old school, from 1910," said Scott. "The only other one I've heard of is in—"

"Fort Knox," finished Luis. The news was a blow. "You don't have time to crack that lock. It's too tough."

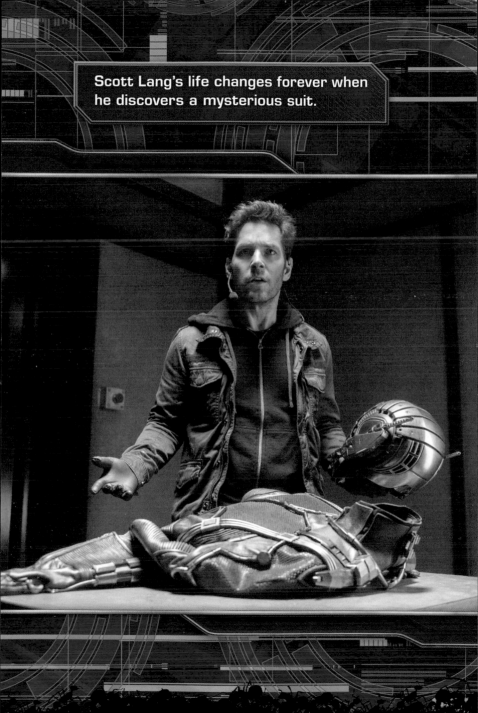

Scott Lang's life changes forever when he discovers a mysterious suit.

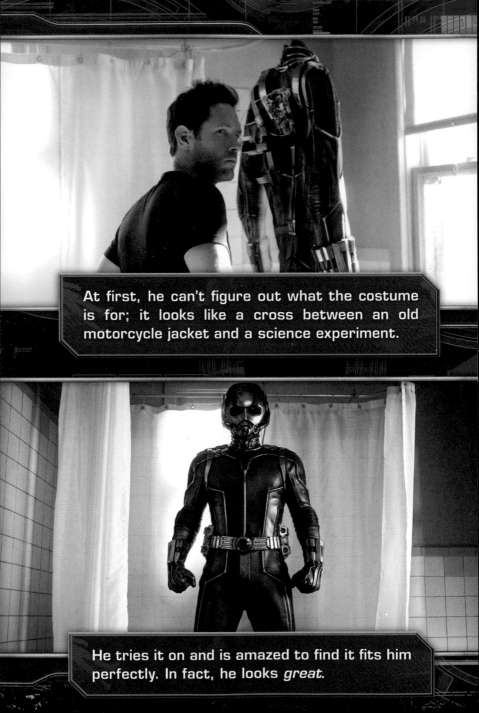

At first, he can't figure out what the costume is for; it looks like a cross between an old motorcycle jacket and a science experiment.

He tries it on and is amazed to find it fits him perfectly. In fact, he looks *great*.

It's then that Scott accidentally discovers the suit can shrink him down to the size of an ant!

Soon Scott learns that, many years ago, a man named Hank Pym invented the suit.

He hid it away to protect the world from those who would abuse the technology.

Hank explains that he's chosen Scott to continue his work now.

Scott must become Ant-Man.

He'll work alongside Hank and his daughter, Hope Van Dyne.

Hank and Hope will teach Scott how to operate the suit—which, besides shrinking, gives him the ability to communicate with ants!

With these powers and his own set of skills, Ant-Man protects the world from evil!

Scott examined the vault, rubbing his chin thoughtfully for a second.

"I'm going to give it a shot," Scott said, pulling a canister of nitrogen from his shoulder bag.

"How you gonna do that?" asked Luis.

Scott was scouting through the basement. He located an inflatable mattress and set it to auto-inflate right in front of the vault door.

"It's made from steel, just like the *Titanic*," Scott explained.

"Here's the thing…Steel's not so good in the cold. Remember what the iceberg did?"

Scott got busy. He used his portable drill to drive several small holes in the surface of the safe around the lock mechanism. Then he took a water bottle from his pack, took a sip, and spit streams of water into the freshly drilled holes. Finally he sprayed the nitrogen from

his canister into the holes as well.

"What are you doing?" Dave asked.

"I'm pouring water in the locking mechanism and freezing it with nitrogen," said Scott matter-of-factly, as if it were the most commonplace activity in the world.

When that was done, he looked around again, found an old recliner, and pulled it near the safe, ducking behind it.

"What are you doing now?" Dave asked.

"Waiting," he said.

Suddenly—BANG! One of the bolts from the safe door shot off, slamming into the back of the recliner. The force of the expanding water inside the mechanism was warping the steel of the vault, forcing it to buckle.

BANG! BANG! BANG! BANG! After another series of exploding bolts, the safe door

creaked…and then fell, landing on—and popping—the inflatable mattress. The mattress had acted as a cushion, muffling the sound of the heavy metal door falling.

Scott walked up to the vault and now easily spun the tumblers, opening the inner door. He peered inside, eager to finally discover what this big prize they'd all been working for was going to turn out to be.

He was surprised. Not in a good way.

"Oh, come on!" he nearly shouted. "It's a motorcycle suit?"

"What'd you say?" asked Luis.

"There's nothing here."

"What? No cash? No jewels?"

Scott looked more closely at the contents of the vault. It was some kind of retro-looking leather bodysuit with an oddly shaped helmet.

"No, just some weird suit. The whole job's a bust!"

There was a moment of silence on the line as it sank in for all the men that their huge score had come to nothing.

"Well, just grab it and get out of there," said Luis to Scott.

Scott nodded to himself and started grabbing pieces of the suit off its rack, shoving them into his bag.

"When it rains, it pours," he said to himself, reflecting on his wave of bad luck.

Scott didn't know it, but, three floors up, Hank Pym was watching a live video feed of the basement on a security monitor that was

connected to the house's closed-circuit television system.

He had sat there, silently witnessing every move Scott had made since coming onto the grounds…and the look on his face didn't seem too displeased.

He took another sip of his drink as he watched Scott make his getaway.

CHAPTER 7

hile Scott and his friends were dealing with the fact that their big heist had turned out to be a failure, Darren Cross was on the verge of success on the other side of the city.

He motioned for his lab techs to load the next lamb into the experimental target area. He knew he was close. It was just a matter of balancing the wavelength alignments. He would get it; he was sure of it.

When the lamb was in position behind a protective glass structure, Darren turned on the device again....

But this time the lamb wasn't harmed.

It just...shrank!

Darren approached the target area, leaned down, and gently picked up the now miniaturized lamb.

He smiled.

The techs cheered.

He'd done it.

Many had told him it was impossible.

Pym had told him it was possible but wouldn't help him do it.

But now he had done it without anyone's help.

He was going to be a very, very rich and very, very powerful man.

Pym Tech was an OK name for a company, but Cross Tech sounded even better.

Back at Luis's apartment, the disappointed team trooped in, still clearly upset.

"I don't get it," said Luis, throwing himself down on the couch. "That was supposed to have been big for us."

"That was a big, fat pain, yes?" asked Kurt, pacing around, angry.

"It was still fun hanging out," said Dave, trying to look on the bright side.

They all looked at him blankly. None of the rest of them was ready to look on the bright side.

"Shut up, Dave," growled Luis.

"I'm going to go take a shower," Scott

announced, walking from the room, his bag in tow.

Once he got to the bathroom, he shut the door, locked it, and ripped the suit out of his bag. He started inspecting it piece by piece, trying to figure out what the old man could possibly have thought was so important about it that he would put it under that kind of security.

"So weird," he said to himself, as he inspected the stitching. There was something strange about the suit. When he looked closely he could see what looked like webbing or an interlocked network of tiny hoses. And the strange-shaped helmet. What could that be all about?

He saw two canister-like structures, one blue, one red, but he had no idea what function they could possibly serve.

Of course, there was one way to check the costume out.

He could always try it on.

Nah…no way. Put on some random, clearly ancient outfit that a crazy old man kept in his basement? Who knew where it had been?

Yes, if there's one thing Scott was sure of, it was that he'd be insane to put on that suit.

So he must have been insane, because the curiosity was killing him.

He put it on.

As he finished, he tried to see himself, but the mirror was too small.

Luis knocked on the bathroom door. "Yo, Lang, hurry it up. It's bath time. I'm starting to get funky."

"I'm changing," said Scott, still staring at himself in the little mirror.

"Let me in," came Luis's reply.

"I don't know about that," said Scott, stepping back into the bathtub, just so he'd be far enough from the mirror to see more of his body in it. He had to admit, for a weird old costume, he actually looked kind of good in it. Strange, but good.

In simpler times, Scott and Cassie used to always joke about what it'd be like if they could be Super Heroes like Captain America, Iron Man, Thor, and the other Avengers. Cassie used to always say how cool it would be to see him in a Super Hero costume. Scott was reminded of that, looking at himself in this getup.

Another knock. "Yo, Scott! Come on, man! Hurry up!"

Looking it over, Scott noticed a small red button, like a trigger, in the right-hand glove of the suit.

Yeah…everyone knows that whatever you do, you should *never* push the random red button. But Scott's fascination overwhelmed him, and he hit it.

It felt as if some kind of fluid was suddenly rushing into the tube network built into the suit.

Suddenly, the room flashed with red light, and Scott was gone.

A second later, a blue light flashed, and Scott was back.

In that second he had shrunk! He freaked out and felt his chest heaving, his heart racing. It was the craziest thing he'd ever experienced. From his point of view, it was like the whole room had suddenly grown huge!

"Time's up, I'm coming in," shouted Luis. The door started to open.

Scott, now only half an inch high, looked

around at the sides of the dirty bathtub he'd been standing in. They looked like massive canyon walls!

Everything around him seemed like it belonged to an alien landscape. Stray fingernail clippings seemed more like dinosaur spines. Loose human hairs looked like strands of rope. The lime streaks around the tub gave the appearance of being geological strata in a mountainside.

Scott could hear the sound of Luis walking into the room. "Scott, where'd you go?" he asked, pulling back the shower curtain.

Scott looked up at the massive Luis, towering above him like a giant from a fable.

"Seriously, where'd you go, Scotty?" Luis asked again, confused.

Luis looked around again but, seeing nothing, just shrugged and went to turn on the water.

To Scott, the rush of water coming out of the faucet seemed like Niagara Falls. When the water hit the surface of the tub, it made a huge wave, headed straight for Scott!

This had been a dumb idea, he realized, seeing the water speeding toward him in what was, for him at this size, a tidal wave.

He quickly pressed the blue button, expecting to grow back up to regular size, but instead the trigger just sparked and the blue light flickered. "Oh, come on! Don't be broken!" Scott pleaded… but it clearly was.

The water would wash him away within seconds, so Scott tried the only thing he could think to do. He tried jumping away from it.

Suddenly—*woooosh*—he leaped far into the air with an unfeasible amount of power! He shot right out of the tub and traveled an arc in the air half the length of the bathroom before landing in an uncontrolled roll on the floor.

"Arughhh!" Scott managed, trying to stop himself as he continued to roll into a crack in the floorboard. He tumbled through the crack, spilling out of a hole in the water-damaged ceiling of the apartment below Luis's and slamming into the surface below.

Scott moaned, pulling himself off the floor. He expected to have broken every bone in his body, but instead he seemed fine. The fall hadn't hurt him at all!

But deafening music blasted all around him. He looked down to see that he'd landed on a rapidly moving black surface. When Scott saw a giant needle hurtling toward him like a speeding truck, he realized he was on a record turntable!

Scott leaped off, sailing through the room past

giant dancing bodies. He landed on the floor near the stomping of giant dancing shoes. Scott ran, evading the crushing power of all those rising and falling footsteps.

Finally, he made it to the apartment's closed front door, and slipped under it, into the hallway...where he was immediately sucked up into a giant dust storm! The neighbor lady was vacuuming, and Scott was now being slammed around inside the vacuum's mechanism. He absorbed a few strong impacts before being shot out into the dust bag.

Soon the lady stopped to dump the full bag, and the second she unzipped it, Scott, coughing from all the dust, leaped!

He shot straight out of the bag, trailing dust behind him like a comet...and right into the face of a *giant rat*!

The rodent charged him, snapping and biting!

Scott ran quickly and stepped right into a trap! But when the hammer released, it catapulted Scott into the air like a bullet, busting him through the glass of the apartment window and out into the rainy night.

Sailing through the night sky, Scott was amazed to see raindrops the size of his head falling all around him.

Seconds later, Scott crashed onto the roof of a car, making a little impact dent in the metal. The impact jarred loose the stuck blue button, and Scott suddenly *grew* back to normal size!

Scott stood still, trying to breathe, trying to calm down. He looked around, letting himself

process everything that had happened to him in the past couple of minutes.

He supposed he should have been scared. Or freaked out, or something…but instead he was nothing but excited.

"That was awesome," he said breathlessly to himself.

Basically, he'd just gotten a superpower. Oh yeah…this was going to be fun.

CHAPTER 8

Soon, Scott was spending a lot of time in Luis's bathroom with the door locked, seeking the privacy he needed to work on the suit. He not only fixed the wiring to the blue button, but also replaced and refurbished several other parts. He still didn't know what the red and blue stuff was, or how the suit granted him the amazing power that it did, but he did know electrical systems well enough that he could maintain them without necessarily understanding all aspects of their function.

Scott's mind was constantly racing, thinking of things he could do with the suit…with the shrinking power. The possibilities were endless. He had so many great ideas that he was going to have to prioritize.

*Okay, first things first….*He needed to make enough cash to stabilize his life and give himself a chance to see Cassie again. That seemed like an insurmountable problem a few days ago, but now, thanks to the suit, it was easy. All he had to do was combine his electrical engineering skills with his newfound power.

Heading to an ATM on the other side of the city, Scott shrank down and jumped up to the face of the machine, quickly finding a place to slip

inside the outer casing. Once he'd wormed his way to the internal circuits, it took only a few minutes to rewire things so that the program would respond to a PIN code that he programmed.

Going back outside and sizing back up, all Scott had to do was press his four-number code into the ATM, and—*ta-da*! The machine starting spitting out every single bill it held. Scott walked away with the entire cash contents of the ATM.

Instant payday!

That night, Maggie came home to find Scott waiting for her at her house. She walked up to him slowly, nervous about what he could possibly be up to.

"What are you doing here, Scott?" she asked in a wary tone.

"You know all that child support I owe you?" he asked.

"Yeah?" she said. "What about it?"

"Here it is."

He handed her a stack of cash.

She took the money automatically but looked down at it, amazed.

"And here's the next year's worth of child support," he said, handing her another stack of cash.

She was stunned, looking at Scott and saying nothing.

"Oh, yeah, and here's a video game console," Scott said, handing Maggie a shopping bag.

"But—but—but—" Maggie stammered.

Scott just smiled. "Good night, Maggie," said Scott, walking away.

That felt good.

But it didn't stop there.

Scott figured that if the suit could help him, it

could help his friends, too. Scott wasn't yet ready to tell anyone—not even Luis—about the suit or what it could do, partly because he could barely believe it himself. But still, he decided to find a way to help Luis and the others without them realizing he'd done it.

The next time Luis, Dave, and Kurt headed for the casino, Scott shrank down and followed them, jumping onto the van as they drove away. Once there, Scott, still small, followed them around and did things to help them win at their games.

When Luis rolled dice, Scott was secretly there, turning the dice over to the number Luis needed to win. The guys were thrilled to think that they were on a winning streak that couldn't be stopped, never suspecting that Scott was helping them win. Each of them left with a stack of cash!

Back at the apartment, Luis, Dave, and Kurt came in to find Scott innocently sitting on the couch, pretending like he hadn't had to furiously race them to get to the apartment first. Only seconds before, he had changed out of his shrinking suit and jumped over to the couch, trying to make it look as if he'd been there all night long.

The guys came in, showing off their winnings and dealing bills out into the air. The money fell around them.

Scott smiled at seeing them happy for the first time since the failed heist. And he was proud to know that he was the one who had put those smiles on their faces.

Another thing he could do with the suit was to go see Cassie.

She couldn't see him, of course, but Scott, while

ant-sized, could visit her at school or at home and find tiny hiding places where he'd stay unseen. It wasn't as good as actually getting to spend time with her, but at least he could observe her from time to time and make sure she was okay.

It was while watching her at school that Scott first saw the bully.

Cassie was playing dodge ball in gym class with the other kids, when one of the larger boys pegged her with the ball, hitting her much harder than he needed to and enjoying it. Cassie, now "out," turned to walk off the court, but Scott saw the bully again raise a ball high, like he was going to hit Cassie in the back!

Not very sporting of him...

Just as the bully released the ball, Scott leaped through the air and slammed into it! None of the kids understood what happened, but suddenly the ball bounced backward and slammed into the bully who'd thrown it, half knocking him down!

But that wasn't the last time the bully went after Cassie.

Later, after school, Cassie was minding her own business and playing with the stuffed animal Scott had gotten her for his birthday, when the bully walked up to her.

"Oh, look. The little baby has a dolly," said the Bully, mocking her.

Cassie tried to leave, but the bully grabbed her stuffed animal. Since he was much taller than her, he held it over her head, taunting her. She leaped for it but couldn't reach it. The bully laughed and acted like he was going to throw Cassie's favorite toy in the trash before Cassie finally was able to grab it back and run away.

Watching her go, the bully laughed.

Only minutes later, when the bully was alone in the school hallway, Scott suddenly grew to normal size right in front of him, appearing as if from nowhere, and shouted, "Leave Cassie alone!"

Scott instantly shrank, disappearing from view again. The bully didn't seem so tough as he ran away screaming.

Scott smiled. He was able to protect his little girl.

It might have been a small victory over a school-age bully, but it felt good to be on the winning side again.

Scott realized that he couldn't keep doing his ATM trick to get money.

First of all, even though it was just stealing from a big bank, it was still stealing…and Scott had wanted—had *promised* himself—that he would turn his life around. Even if he was having a little trouble keeping that promise lately, he knew Cassie deserved a father who wasn't a criminal. So, he was going to keep trying to be good.

And besides, it might take a while, but there was always the possibility of getting caught and going back to San Quentin.

So, no more ATMs…

But surely there had to be something he could use the suit for to get himself a solid chunk of cash, right?

He was thinking about this as he walked by a convenience store that advertised the lottery. "Tickets sold here," the sign noted. There was a

big draw coming, with a pot in the millions.

Scott looked at that sign for a beat, then realized what he needed to do. He walked inside and bought a ticket with random numbers.

A few days later, the lottery commission pulled the winners on live TV. Viewers at home held their tickets hopefully, watching as a smiling woman pulled random numbered balls out of an air-driven hopper one by one.

What you couldn't see by watching on-screen was that inside that hopper was a little man trying to grab on to the balls and redirect them up the selection tube.

To Scott, ant-sized, the blowing air inside the hopper was like a tornado!

He bravely jumped around inside, constantly getting smashed by balls—but sorting through them and grabbing the ones he needed, in the

order he needed, to make his ticket become the winner.

The first ball was easy. Scott was sure he could do this.

The second ball nearly got away from him, but he was able to grab it and send it up.

He almost wasn't fast enough to get the third ball in, but by slamming away another one at the last minute he was able to do it.

Three…two…six…The TV hostess pulled Scott's numbers. He was going to do this! All he had to do was get the number one ball into the final position—

But when the woman drew the last ball, it was a seven!

Scott had failed, unable to find the number one ball fast enough.

He crept out of the studio, went back to Luis's

apartment, and ripped up his *losing* lottery ticket.

OK, maybe not every idea was going to work out, but still, Scott could think of plenty of stuff that he could pull off.

In fact, there was something he'd always wanted to do....

CHAPTER 9

Jim Paxton sat at his desk at the station, minding his own business, working on some files, when a paper clip slapped him in the forehead. It stung!

"Ouch!" he shouted, looking up, trying to see where it had come from. All he could see was his partner, Gale, across the desk from him.

"Dude!" Paxton said to Gale.

"What?" Gale asked innocently. He had no

idea what was bothering Paxton.

Paxton shrugged and looked back down at his file.

Snap! It happened again! Another flying paper clip?

Paxton rubbed a red welt that was beginning to rise on his forehead.

"Come on! Who's doing that?" said Paxton, reeling around, trying to spot his attacker. No one was around!

He couldn't see, on a nearby shelf, the shrunken-down Scott, laughing. A load of paper clips sat stacked next to an improvised launcher built out of pushpins and rubber bands.

Yeah, this was as good as Scott hoped it would be.

Snap!

"Seriously, where are those coming from?!"

As he walked down the street enjoying a smoothie that he'd bought at full price, Scott had to admit that he was feeling pretty good.

He may not have been able to "win" the lottery, but with these powers, Scott had caught up on his debts, protected his daughter, and had some fun....

He was starting to feel something he hadn't felt since before going to prison....It had been so long that he barely remembered what this emotion was called, but it might have been "hope."

That's when Scott saw something nice and shiny across the street.

It was an armored truck.

Scott stopped and watched the armed guards

carefully and efficiently loading locked containers from the side of a bank into the truck.

Right off the top of his head, Scott could think of six different ways to use the shrink-suit to burglarize that truck, stripping it of all cash without anyone getting hurt.

It wouldn't be that big a deal, right?

The only victim would be some big, faceless corporate bank....

Yeah, it was something to think about.

Scott was still thinking about it that night when he went to watch Cassie's bedtime.

Maggie was putting Cassie to bed, tucking her in as she clutched the ugly stuffed animal that Scott had bought her in Chinatown. An ant-

sized Scott hid nearby and watched.

"Are you sure you don't want to sleep with another stuffed animal?" Maggie asked.

"No, I love this one," Cassie said sweetly.

Maggie frowned but didn't object. "Okay. Have a good night, bug," said Maggie.

As Maggie reached to turn out the light, Cassie looked up at her. The little girl had an expression of concern written across her face.

"Momma?"

"What is it, bug?"

"Is Daddy—is he…bad?" asked Cassie weakly.

Hearing the question made Scott's heart drop.

Maggie paused for a second. "What makes you ask that, honey?"

"I heard some grown-ups talking," Cassie explained. "They said he was bad."

Maggie took this in, thinking of the best

response. "Your father just gets confused sometimes," she said finally.

Cassie thought about this but didn't reply. Maggie gave her another kiss good night and turned off the light, leaving Cassie in the dark to fall asleep.

And leaving Scott in the dark, too.

At first he was angry. He wanted to find out who had said things like that about him around his daughter, and use his shrink powers to make them pay....

But "making people pay" wouldn't exactly convince them that he wasn't bad, like they said he was.

No, Scott realized that he wasn't really mad at the people who had said that; he was mad at himself, for living a life that could be talked about in that way.

"What do you think?" came a deep voice. "Are you a bad man?"

The voice came from out of nowhere and shocked Scott! At first he looked around, thinking that another tiny man might be standing just behind him. Then he thought it might be a full-sized person in the room with him…but no, no one was there, either.

Then he realized, it was a voice *inside* his helmet!

Scott raced back to Luis's apartment, leaping up and entering from the outside. He went straight into the bathroom. Once inside, he quickly sized back up to normal, then ripped at the suit. He couldn't get it off soon enough.

Someone was tracking him with the suit, and they knew where his daughter lived.

He had to get rid of it.

But he couldn't just drop it in a trash can somewhere. What if a *real* criminal got hold of the suit?

He knew what he had to do. He had to sneak it back into Pym's house, back to where he'd found it. That was the only way to be sure that it was safe.

Once the suit was off, he threw it in a bag and headed out. Walking by, he ran into Luis, Dave, and Kurt.

"Hey, bro, we're headed back out to the casino," called out Luis. "We gotta ride this hot streak we're on."

"I'd quit while you were ahead," mumbled Scott, rushing past them.

118

He was at Pym's house in thirty minutes and had broken inside in another five. He made his way back down to the basement and, not knowing what else to do, he left the suit inside the safe, which still had its door blown off.

With the suit returned, Scott went back up into the house, then slipped out through a side window, but just as he did...

Lights came on everywhere! Scott was surrounded by five squad cars and at least a dozen cops!

"Get down on the ground! You are under arrest!" one of the cops shouted through a megaphone.

Scott did as he was told, but shouted back, "No...I wasn't stealing anything! I was returning something I stole...!"

But after a second, he realized, "That doesn't sound good, does it?"

eing handcuffed. Having his rights read to him. Being thrown in the back of a car and taken to the station. Being booked. The mug shots. The fingerprinting. It was all so familiar and all so horrible.

He soon found himself inside a holding cell, facing his ex-wife's new fiancé, Jim Paxton.

Of course he would be here. Now Scott's shame and misery were complete.

"You almost had us convinced you were going to change your ways," said Paxton, almost sounding sad. "Maggie and Cassie were really rooting for you. Now I have to go back and tell

them. It'll break their hearts."

Scott looked up at Paxton.

He was right. This was going to break his daughter's heart.

Paxton's partner, Gale, entered the room. "Lang's lawyer's here," he said to Paxton.

Scott got a confused expression on his face. "My lawyer?" he asked.

That's funny. Scott didn't have a lawyer. And even if he did, he hadn't yet had a chance to call anyone. How did some lawyer even know he was here?

Gale motioned for him to stand up, so he did. He was off to meet this "lawyer."

Gale escorted Scott into the interview room, with Scott having no idea what to expect. Yet even with no expectations, it was still a surprise to see Dr. Henry Pym sitting there waiting for him.

"I'm starting to think you prefer the inside of a jail cell," said the older man.

"Oh no," muttered Scott.

The figure now bore little resemblance to the man Scott had seen at Pym's house. He was dressed in the most expensive suit Scott had seen in years. He was groomed and coiffed and looked like a million bucks. Gone was the cane and the large, obvious hearing aid. He was a far cry from the doddering old man in the unlaundered robe who'd roamed through that musty, crowded living room.

In fact, there was such a stark difference that Scott had to ask himself if it really was him, or if it was perhaps a twin brother who had been more committed to a lifetime of healthy living.

But no, it was him for sure. Scott could see the same edgy look in his eyes.

Gale walked out, leaving Scott and Pym alone to talk.

"Sit down," Pym said, a commanding tone in his voice.

"Sir, I'm very sorry I took your suit. I know what it does, and I don't even want to know why you have it," said Scott. "But I promise, I was returning it. I—"

"Shut up," said Pym, cutting Scott off mid-sentence.

Scott was shocked when he saw, over Pym's shoulder, an army of black ants climbing the walls of the interrogation room, headed toward the mounted security cameras. The ants reached the lenses and covered them up with their swarm of bodies. The cameras had in effect been temporarily disabled.

"You're a hopeless case, aren't you?" said Pym, leveling a disarming gaze at Scott.

"What do you mean?" Why was the old man

125

talking to him like this, as if he knew him? More to the point, why was he here claiming to be Scott's attorney?

"You finally get out of prison, you finally get a chance to be in your daughter's life, and what do you do? The moment things get hard, you turn right back to crime. It's pathetic." Pym glowered with disapproval, before continuing. "Maggie was right about you."

Scott was shrinking in his chair, utterly helpless to fend off this verbal attack. Each of Pym's words hit him with the strength of truth.

"No wonder Maggie's trying to keep you away from Cassie," Pym said. "Cassie's better off without a dad like you around."

Hearing that was like taking a punch to the gut. Scott audibly gasped.

"I...I know," he said softly, his eyes glassy.

Seeing his words were having an effect, Pym straightened up, squaring his shoulders.

"The way I see it, you have a choice: You can either spend the rest of your life in prison…or you can go back to your cell and wait for further instructions."

Scott looked up at this, confused. "I don't understand."

Pym frowned.

"No, I don't expect you to," said Pym evenly. "But you don't have a lot of options right now, and quite frankly, neither do I. Why do you think I let you steal that suit in the first place?"

Scott gaped at Pym.

Did he say he "let" Scott steal the suit?

Suddenly, it all became clear.

Why else would a cleaning lady be allowed down in the basement, past the thumbprint-lock door, to see the mother of all safes?

How else would choice info about a possible break-in job, one that exactly fits Scott's MO, happen to fall right into the lap of Scott's own roommate the very week that Scott was released from prison?

Add to it the whole "tipping him a quarter" thing, clearly designed to infuriate him and goad him into going through with the burglary.

And the doddering-old-man routine, which Scott could now clearly see was a lie....

And the voice he'd heard in the helmet of the costume...

It all pointed to one inescapable conclusion: Scott had been played.

And he'd fallen for it hook, line, and sinker.

Why hadn't he seen it before?

He looked at the old man in a whole new light.

Pym leaned in, his voice a little softer now. "Second chances don't come around all that much," he said with the tone of someone giving advice to a friend. "So, the time you think you might see one, I suggest you take a real close look at it."

With that, Pym stood up and walked out of the room.

Scott watched him go, feeling like he was trying to catch his balance…like the whole earth had moved under his feet.

Gale walked back into the room. "Back to lockup, jerk," he said.

Scott stood up automatically, his actions mechanical. He was still in shock.

Escorted by Gale, he shuffled back to his cell.

He was still processing the mysterious meeting with Pym when another line of ants came marching in, under the door of his cell. They seemed to be carrying something—was it doll's clothing?

Scott looked more closely when the thing suddenly enlarged. It was the shrink-suit! The one he'd stolen from and returned to Pym's house!

Scott grabbed the suit and stared at it. What was going on?

That's when he saw the ants moving together into formation on the ground. Together they made the shape of a ten....Then they moved—a nine...Then an eight...

Scott got the idea. It was a countdown.

He hurriedly put on the suit. He hit the button before the ants even made it to one and instantly shrank down to their size.

Outside in the hallway, Gale was pacing,

keeping guard. When he reached Scott's cell, he looked in—and had to do a double take. Then he started freaking out and radioed for help....

Because the cell was empty!

Or so it seemed.

Insect-size and hiding in the shadows, Scott watched as the—from his perspective—giant Gale shouted in alarm.

Over the helmet earpiece, Scott could hear Pym's voice speaking. "Smart choice, putting on the suit. Okay, I'm going to walk you through this, so no need to panic. This is very important: You're about to have some very strange experiences, Scott. Don't forget to breathe, and stay calm."

Scott nodded, collecting his wits.

The voice continued, "Now, walk out of that cell and turn right."

Scott followed the directions, running under the door, under Gale's legs, and out into the hallway. Alarms were going off all around him, but Scott tried to focus. He ran through the crowded hallway, which was filling up with running, stomping feet! At his size, the footsteps fell around him with the sound of bombs going off.

He could hear Paxton, his voice booming from above, shouting, "Where'd he go?"

Gale's voice responded, "I don't know; he just disappeared!"

"Set up a five-block perimeter!" shouted Paxton, clearly upset.

As Scott got to the end of the hallway, Pym said, "Now you're going to turn right and go under that door. You'll be outside."

Scott did as he was told, and almost ran

straight into a giant cockroach! Okay, so the roach wasn't giant—Scott was small—but it was still terrifying. Scott dodged the bug and saw it scuttling off. He realized it was just as afraid of him as he was of it.

But when Scott turned around again, he nearly ran into a bunch of ants, all standing in a precise, military-like line.

"Ahhh!" Scott shouted at the ants. Looking around, he quickly found a stray match discarded on the ground. It was almost the size of his body. He grabbed it and ran the head along the ground, lighting it.

"Get back!" shouted Scott, brandishing the match like a fiery torch.

"Scott, these are my associates," said Pym's voice.

"Associates?" asked Scott. He looked more

closely. The center ant had a camera mounted on its head. "A camera on an ant? Sure, why not? Okay....Where's the car?"

"No car," said Pym. "We got wings."

The camera ant stepped forward, unfolding its wings. It suddenly looked magnificent, like a big winged horse. It even wore a saddle.

"Put your foot on the central node and mount the thorax," instructed Pym.

"You made it a saddle? How safe is—?" Scott started to ask.

"Get on the ant!" shouted Pym.

Scott shrugged and did what he was told.

The ant suddenly took off into the air! It raced Scott out above the police station, above the scattering squad cars, and out into the city.

As the ant rose high, Scott could look around at the buildings.

It was a breathtaking view, the city stretched before him.

Scott had no idea what was coming next, but right now he was miniaturized and riding on top of a bug. He had to admit, it was panic-inducing, it was even terrifying...but it was also kind of fun.

It was like when he'd given Cassie that strange toy for her birthday. He could almost hear his daughter's voice in his mind, saying, "So weird and great!"

Whatever was coming his way, Scott was sure it was going to be a mix of weird...and great....

EPILOGUE

Scott would always remember those events as the time when his life changed forever.

The next day, Pym brought Scott further into his confidence. Pym himself had invented the shrinking powers that the suit used. Many had wanted to harness that power, but fearing it would be abused, Pym hid the power away.

Darren Cross, once Pym's assistant, had

learned about the existence of that technology, and wanted it—but when Pym wouldn't give it to him, Cross forced him out of Pym Tech, Pym's own company. It became clear that Cross wanted the secrets of miniaturization for his own nefarious purposes.

Pym's daughter, Hope, had a complicated and uncomfortable history with her father; but once she realized that Darren Cross's bid for power was dangerous, she teamed up with her father in an attempt to block Darren from using her father's technology for evil.

Pym and Hope needed Scott. They needed his skills, and they needed him to operate the suit.

Pym asked Scott to become "Ant-Man"—a hero who would use his shrinking powers to stop the plans of evil men like Darren Cross.

It was something that Scott couldn't walk

away from, not if it meant that he could make the world a safer place for his daughter and others.

He had to take it.

Besides, he knew that if he could become a hero—a *true* hero—it would help erase his past and allow him to be the kind of man—the kind of father—that Cassie deserved for him to be.

Yes, Scott Lang became Ant-Man!